Written by Dyan Beyer
Illustrated by Brianalise Marie

Copyright © 2024 by Dyan Beyer

ISBN: 978-1-77883-515-5 (Paperback)

All rights reserved. No part of this publication may be reproduced, distributed, or transmitted in any form or by any means, including photocopying, recording, or other electronic or mechanical methods, without the prior written permission of the publisher, except in the case brief quotations embodied in critical reviews and other noncommercial uses permitted by copyright law.

The views expressed in this book are solely those of the author and do not necessarily reflect the views of the publisher, and the publisher hereby disclaims any responsibility for them. Some names and identifying details in this book have been changed to protect the privacy of individuals.

BookSide Press
877-741-8091
www.booksidepress.com
orders@booksidepress.com

To all six of my blessings

George
Bear
Grace
Paul
Creed
Ruth

Written in honor of my newest grandchild, Ruth Christine Beyer

Other books by Dyan Beyer

Under Angels' Wings
Baby Boy Bear
Baby Grace Is Here!
Baby Needs Pants
Little Lion
Bear And The Dinosaur
The 5 Wise Grandchildren
George's Pup

Buddy, the horse, lived on a farm with a goat without a name. He was just called Goat. They played together every day in the pasture. Buddy always told the truth but Goat, did not!

Goat would always tell Buddy something that wasn't always true. He would tell Buddy things like, 'Buddy it's cold outside so you better wear your blanket!' Buddy would go outside the barn and it would not be cold but instead it would be very HOT! Or he would tell Buddy that the corn was really tasty and he should try it. Buddy went over to the cornfield and took a big bite of corn, spitting it out because it was not yet ready to eat! Buddy tried to explain to Goat that it wasn't a good thing to lie but the goat didn't believe him.

"Hey Buddy, those kids that live up the street are at the gate with carrots for you!" Goat said.

"Is Ruth with them?" Buddy asked. He particularly liked little Ruth because she always scratched his neck as she fed him carrots.

"Yep, Ruth's with them! And all her siblings and her cousins are out there waiting for you!" Buddy believed Goat and ran all through the pasture to get to the gate believing his friends were waiting there for him. When he got there, he realized that Goat was lying once again!

He could hear Goat laughing behind him. Buddy didn't think that Goat was very nice. Buddy went back up to the barn disappointed that he didn't get to see the kids. But he was more disappointed about Goat telling him another lie!

On another day, Goat came into the barn to tell Buddy that the farmer sold him to another farm. Crying, Buddy ran out of his stall to see if the horse trailer was there to take him away. Goat came running out after him laughing, thinking it was funny that Buddy believed another one of his lies!

The next day Goat asked Buddy if he would like to go out in the pasture and run around with him. Buddy really liked to run so he agreed to go with Goat. They ran around and played and then Buddy noticed the kids coming down the street. He quickly left Goat and galloped to the gate to greet his friends.

"Hey, wait for me!" Goat yelled as he followed behind Buddy.

Goat watched from afar as Ruth and the kids fed and petted Buddy. Goat was sad that the kids gave Buddy a name and he didn't have one. The kids would just call him Goat. They never would pet him or bring him food. Goat felt left out.

Buddy would neigh and happily shake his head with each treat that was given to him. Whenever Buddy shook his head, the kids would give him another treat. He looked so happy thought Goat! Goat wondered again why no one ever brought him any treats or never pet him! He wondered why the kids would trust Buddy to be their friend but not him!

Back at the barn, Goat decided he would ask Buddy why Ruth and the kids liked him so much and why they didn't pay any attention to him? The goat listened carefully to what Buddy had to say.

"Goat, the kids love me because I'm always very nice to them and thankful when they bring me treats. They trust me because I don't lie to them! But the most important reason is, that they have to trust you before they like you or want to feed you."

"How did you learn all of this, Buddy?" Goat asked.

"I learned what is right and wrong from the Bible. God loves you and wants you to be happy but lying is a sin! 'Lying lips are an abomination to the Lord, but those who act faithfully are his delight.' I want to please God. When you lie, you are really lying to God. And when you lie to others, you lose their trust!

Goat took a moment for Buddy's words to sink in and then he asked, "So when I lie, no one will trust or obey me?"

"Yes that is correct. Think about it, Goat, how can you earn trust when you lie?"

"I guess I can't! I'm sorry I lied to you, Buddy. I won't anymore because I want to be like you!"

The next day when Buddy saw the kids running to the gate he invited Goat to come over with him. At first, the kids were a little unsure of the goat until Goat rubbed his head against their bellies. It took a little while before Goat earned their trust.

In time, the kids started to trust Goat and to obey him when he nudged them to be pet. Then they soon trusted him enough to feed him some carrots. Goat was the most happiest when he heard Ruth say, "This goat is NOW a nice goat and he deserves a name." They decided to call him Peanuts!

From then on, when the kids came, they could be heard calling out for Buddy and Peanuts!

The End

In a meadow green and wide stood a goat and horse, side by side. Friends they were, or so it seemed but little did, Buddy, the horse know it was all just a dream. The goat would tell lies to the horse, thinking lying would make him the boss! The goat's deceitful words caused great dismay. Obeying God was the only way. The goat was confronted and made to see that lying was harmful, not the way to be! With God's guidance, he learned to be true and his friendships grew. Even his friendship with Buddy was renewed. Now the goat is honest, no longer deceitful, his bond with Buddy is strong and peaceful. Thanks to God's intervention the goat, learned his lesson! His friendship with Buddy is now a possession.

Proverbs 222:6
Start children off on the way they should go, and even when they are old they will not turn from it.